Maybe I Can Love My Neighbor Too

by
Jennifer Grant

illustrated by
Benjamin Schipper

Text copyright © 2019 Jennifer Grant
Illustration copyright © 2019 Beaming Books

Published in 2019 by Beaming Books, an imprint of 1517 Media. All rights reserved. No part of this book may be reproduced without the written permission of the publisher. Email copyright@1517.media. Printed in the United States of America

25 24 23 22 21 20 19   1 2 3 4 5 6 7 8 9

Hardcover ISBN: 9781506452012

Written by Jennifer Grant
Illustrated by Benjamin Schipper
Designed by Joe Reinke, 1517 Media

Library of Congress Cataloging-in-Publication Data

Names: Grant, Jennifer (Jennifer C.) author. | Schipper, Benjamin, illustrator.

Title: Maybe I can love my neighbor too / written by Jennifer Grant ; illustrated by Benjamin Schipper.

Description: First edition. | Minneapolis, MN : Beaming Books, 2019.

Summary: A young girl learns from her mother that everyone is her neighbor and that if she is observant, she can find ways to show love to neighbors near and far.

Identifiers: LCCN 2018050750 | ISBN 9781506452012 (hard cover : alk. paper)

Subjects: | CYAC: Neighbors--Fiction. | Love--Fiction. | Christian life--Fiction. | City and town life--Fiction.

Classification: LCC PZ7.1.G725 Mbi 2019 | DDC [E]--dc23

LC record available at https://lccn.loc.gov/2018050750

VN0004589;9781506452012;FEB2019

Beaming Books
510 Marquette Avenue
Minneapolis, MN 55402
beamingbooks.com

For Ace,
with love
and admiration

—J. G.

"Love your neighbor as yourself."
—Leviticus 19:18

I live at the corner
of 9th and 19th,
upstairs in apartment 4-A.

A building is going up
across the street.
Week after week,
it grows taller and taller,
climbing up high in the sky.

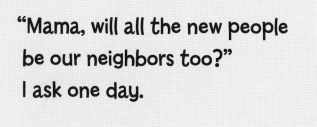

"Mama, will all the new people
be our neighbors too?"
I ask one day.

"Every single person
is our neighbor," she says,
"whether they live next door,
or across the street,
or far, far away."

"I know I'm supposed to love my neighbors,
but how can I love that many people?" I ask.

Mama gives me a hug.
"Oh, honey," she says, "I'm sure you'll find a way!
Maybe start by noticing the ways others show love."

A man walks by the construction site
pushing a shopping cart that's stuffed
with blankets and bags.

The wheels hit a bump in the road
and the cart almost tips over—
but one of the workers moves fast to catch it
and sets it upright again.

Helping someone who's just
passing by is a way to show love.

Maybe I can love my neighbor too.

Mama and I walk down to the park,
just like we do every day.

I see a man and a woman up ahead
talking to people while they wait at the light.

I stare at the pictures on the man's
arms while he tells Mama about people
who had to leave their homes because
they weren't safe anymore.

Mama hands a few dollars to the woman, who has
a purple stripe in her hair.

Giving money so people can have a safe place to
live is a way to show love.
Maybe I can love my neighbor too.

At the park,
an old man is shouting his
dog's name. "Shadow! Shadow!" he calls.

A boy runs after the dog, diving to catch him.
A minute later, Shadow is back with his owner.

The old man says "thank you" over and over and over.

Helping older folks is a way to show love.
Maybe I can love my neighbor too.

"Mama, look at me!" I shout.
And she waves from the bench
under her favorite tree.

When I'm all out of breath,
I sit at the edge of the sandbox,
watching the other kids play.

A girl tosses me a shovel and pail.
Then we build the most elegant castle
and dig a moat around it.
We decorate it with royal flags
made of sticks and seeds and leaves.

"That was kind of that girl," Mama says
when we're walking back home.

"I liked seeing how she loved her neighbor . . .
and the neighbor this time was you!"

Sharing toys with a new friend is a way to show love.
Maybe I can love my neighbor too.

There's sand between my toes,
and Mama says it's time for the tub.

But then we hear a knock at the door.
It's our neighbors from upstairs,
and they baked us a loaf of bread.

Sharing good things to eat is a way to show love.
Maybe I can love my neighbor too.

At dinner, I tell Daddy,
"Guess what? I learned something new today!"

"That's what I like to hear," he says. "What is it?"

"Every person in the whole world is my neighbor," I say.
"And I can love them too!"

"I could give my birthday money to someone who needs it more than me," I say. "Or I could carry groceries or open doors for people who aren't as strong as I am."

I pull up my sleeves and show my muscles.

"There are a lot of ways," I say. "I can be kind to other kids in the park. Or even bake something to share with people in our building."

"I knew you'd find ways to show love to others," Mama says with a smile.

Every other person in the
whole wide world
is my neighbor,

whether they live next door,
or across the street,
or far, far away.

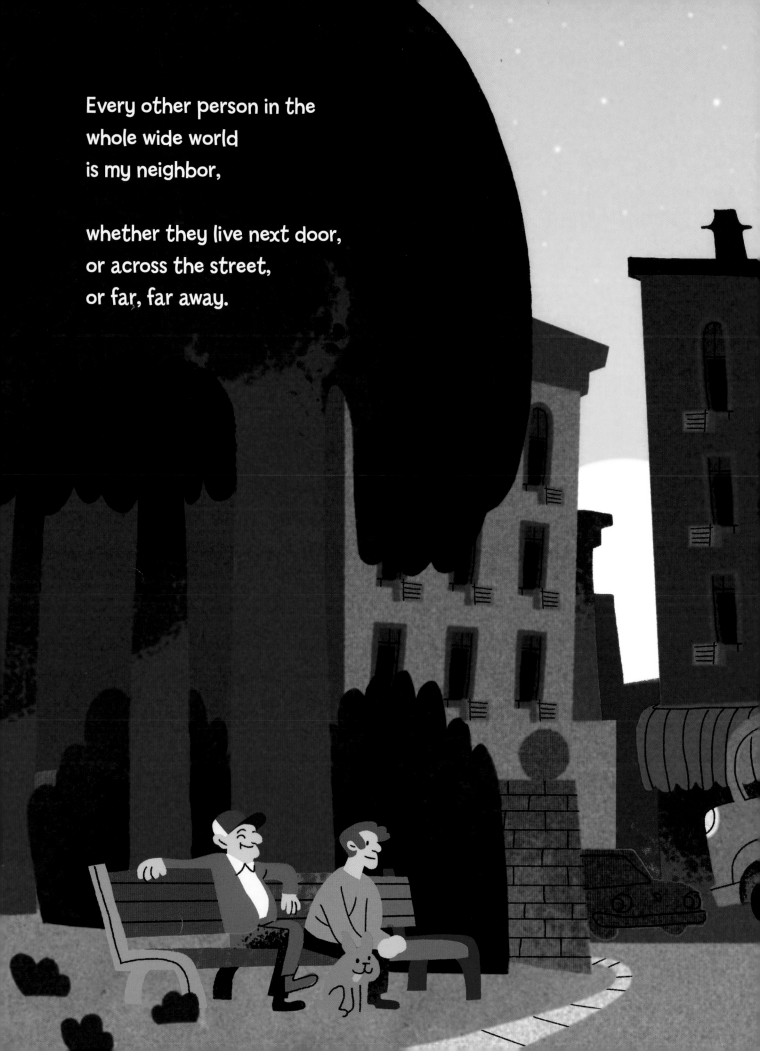

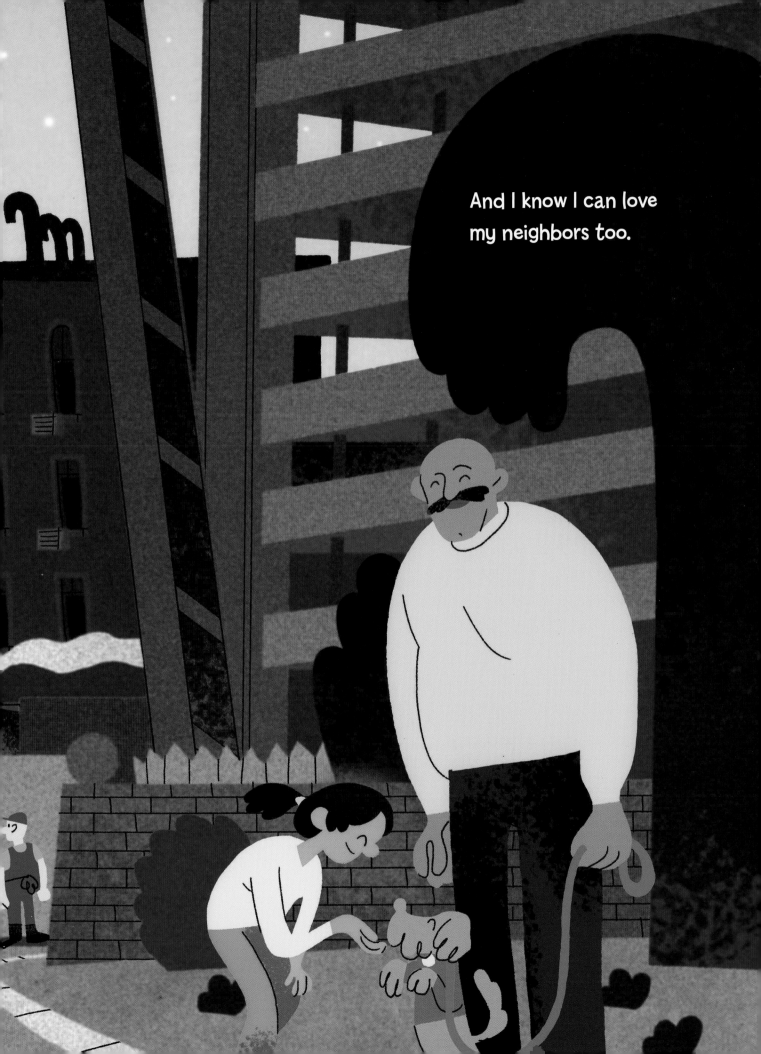

Jennifer Grant

Jennifer Grant is the author of six books for adults, including the adoption memoir *Love You More*, the devotional *Wholehearted Living*, and the midlife memoir *When Did Everybody Else Get So Old?* Her picture book *Maybe God Is Like That Too* won a Moonbeam Spirit gold medal and was named a finalist in the Foreword Indies awards for excellence in children's literature. She is a member of the Society of Children's Book Writers and Illustrators, INK: A Creative Collective, and The Authors Guild. She is the mother of four grown (or nearly-grown) children and lives in the Chicago area with her husband and two rescue dogs. Find her online at jennifergrant.com.

Benjamin Schipper

Benjamin Schipper loves to create artwork and illustrations that have sad, spooky, and poignant emotions. He likes people in general, and animals in particular. He lives in Greenville, South Carolina with his wife, Karen, and their little black dog, Willow.